I0601561

Unsettled
A Short Story

Steve Rzasa

Unsettled by Steve Rzasa
www.steverzasa.com

This is a work of fiction. Names, characters, places, and incidents are products of the author's imagination or are used fictitiously. Any similarity to actual people, organizations, and/or events is purely coincidental.

Cover illustration: Tithi Luadthong (Shutterstock)
Cover design: Steve Rzasa

International Standard Book Number:
9781733585149

Books

Urban Fantasy
>	*Mercury On Guard*
>	*Mercury For Hire*
>	*Mercury At Risk*

Space Opera
>	*The Word Reclaimed: The Face of the Deep 1.0*
>	*The Word Unleashed: The Face of the Deep 2.0*
>	*Broken Sight: The Face of the Deep 2.5*
>	*The Word Endangered: The Face of the Deep 3.0*
>	*Severed Signals*
>	*Cryptic Commands*
>	*Failed Frequencies*
>	*Mixed Messages*
>	*Empire's Rift: A Takamo Universe Novel*
>	*Strife's Cost: A Takamo Universe Novel*

Science-Fiction
>	*Man Behind the Wheel*
>	*Multiverse*
>	*For Us Humans*

Superhero
>	*Airfoil: Origins*

Fantasy
>	*The Bloodheart*
>	*The Lightningfall*
>	*Just Dumb Enough (contributor & editor)*

Steampunk
>	*Crosswind: The First Sark Brothers Tale*
>	*Sandstorm: The Second Sark Brothers Tale*

Timeline of Events
The Face of the Deep

2245
Ardan Verge maintains the Ferro Plains
settlement on Mars

2602
Baden Haczyk aboard *Natalia Zoja* discovers
the last Bible in print

2612
Zarco Thread and surveyor crew of
Cazador stumble upon missing
Starkweather battle corvette

2613
Captain Vincent Chen commanding *RMS
Marconi* investigates comms ferry malfunction
in Sylvanak Star System

2614
Captain Chen searches for a missing spy and
a derelict starship

Chapter One

2245
Ferro Plains
Mars
Sol System

The condenser broke for the third time in six Martian months. Ardan Verge decided he could live without it.

After all, the settlement of Ferro Plains had lost eight people in that time, so the need for what dregs of water could be reclaimed from the rusty regolith declined accordingly. He thought "lost" an unfair term—not to atmo-seal breach, or structural collapse during a dust maelstrom. Not like the men and women of the first-generation settlers.

No, these eight had simply left. Packed up one day and caught the next torch booster into orbit. From there Ardan assumed they'd shipped to a new home, lured by the fleeting glimpses coming down the transmissions across the light-years.

As far as he was concerned, the Raszewski drive was turning Mars into a dead planet all over again.

He spit inside his External Survival suit. Didn't get the grit from between his teeth. It mingled with salty sweat. Nothing got rid of the red dust. Sure, the ES suit sealed tight enough, but he dragged it through the airlock and invariably into the family hab.

Ardan couldn't fault his neighbors for leaving empty habitats, like rabbits on Earth bequeathed warrens. He pulled a superconductor free of the condenser and looked out over the lumps of red dirt arrayed in concentric circles. Aside from a cluster of six-wheeled rovers, and solar panels that followed the anemic sun with unfurling petals, it didn't look like a community. A couple of colonists in white ES suits worked on the solar panels, accompanied by the rolling, yellow and black checkered spheres of Progress Corporation utility drones. Didn't matter. He had sixty people, still, who needed the condensers to stay operational.

"Ard?" The voice crackled in his ES suit's radio. "Any luck?"

"I'm stripping parts off Condenser Four-Seven. We can use them when the other three go down."

"If they go down."

"No, pretty sure it's 'when,' honey."

His wife laughed. Such a warm, human sound.

Nothing like the bleak vista of this, his home world. He shook his head. *Thanks a bunch for getting us stuck here, Grandpa.* "Ard, would you like me to relay that across the settlement channels?"

"Let's keep it to ourselves, Rosie."

"Fine by me. I called to tell you Li Huan left a message."

Ardan tried not to think of the regional administrator sitting in the cooled offices at Boreus Major, fifty klicks northeast. They could lop off as much ice as they needed from the Martian north pole for water. No need to drag dregs from underground, sweating to death in the haze. Ardan pulled cabling free of the defunct condenser and secured the superconductor in the static-sealed bag dangling from his suit. "Give me fifteen minutes and I'll be down the slope."

"All right. Your rad count's at 45 percent."

"I know. It's on the heads-up display."

"And I know you ignore the display when you're focused on a task, so this is a friendly reminder from your communications supervisor." The noise of a blown kiss drifted over the radio. "I passed the message to Tadzio, so you two can listen on the way back. Li's looking for a swift response. Watch your step."

"Listen for my knock." Ardan signed off, grateful for a wife and partner who could keep him mindful of the hostile environment. She was right. For all the weariness he felt as he sprang along in the lesser gravity to the waiting rover, he could lose himself in the vast open space.

"Do you hear this?" Tadeusz Mazorwiecki's thick accent washed out the murmur of a recording over Ardan's radio. "Li Huan is urging us to make best speed to Boreus for a delivery. Has the man no other priorities?"

The rover sagged against six rigged wheels, a bulbous white bug stained ochre and orange. Tadzio, a short, thickset man with wiry brown hair, saluted from the driver's seat.

Ardan swung into the airlock. He slipped from his ES suit as soon as the seals were good, and the cleansers swiped as much dust away as they could. "Play it, Tadzio."

"I already am." Tadzio flicked the volume control with the flourish of a magician bearing his wand.

"…finds you in good health." Li Huan's voice was soft, and mellow. "I would add 'prosperity', but we all know Ferro Plains is in debt. Your holdings have failed to produce the earnings required by Year Sixty of the Verge family contract. What I'm offering is a chance to tip the balance in your favor and reach the settlement goals your grandfather agreed to."

"Lovely," Ardan muttered. "Grandpa would be happy to hear it, if he weren't buried under tons of red left by a maelstrom."

Tadzio shushed him. "This, my friend, is the

good part."

"I have an order for ice, deliverable to the Lore Hotza settlement, within the week. The cargo itself is not problematic, however, the route crosses the Vastitas Flats."

Ardan groaned.

"Your pay, should you succeed, will be fifty thousand apiece."

Tadzio slapped Ardan's jumpsuit. "Fifty thousand! Each! This is the godsend for which we have prayed, Ardan! We do this, we are set."

Ardan switched off the recording. "Are you buried? He said Vastitas!"

"Yes, he did, and so, it will be a rough ride. But the benefits!"

"If we're alive to claim them!" Ardan fired up the rover's power cells. "Vastitas. What does Li think, we have a death wish?"

When Ardan told her Li's offer, Rosie folded her arms. It might as well have been a maelstrom warning on the weathersats.

"Remind me why you're considering *not* taking the job?" she asked.

Ardan threw up his hands. "Because I've got plenty enough to do around here! Ferro Plains isn't top of the line, honey, and it's obvious to everyone but us it's a failing proposition. How many families have left in the past year? The Santiagos, the

Cruzes, the Hanlons, the Learys. We've seen a third of our population go since Dad's time."

"More reason for you to sign on with Li and make this trip, so we can pay off toward the sixty-year mark and put some away for imported parts."

"We should be able to fabricate them, but the printers are glitching." Ardan ran his hand through jagged red hair. He caught sight of his haggard reflection in the glossy black walls of the gravity spinner. The column reached from floor to ceiling of their hab's common room, six meters wide, thrumming with a reassuring vibrato. Reassuring, because its presence meant they could stay acclimated if they ever needed to visit off-world trading posts, which all spun to maintain Earth-compatible gravity. Dad had possessed foresight, in that regard.

"We make do, like we have before." Rosie frowned. "You've never been this concerned about repairs. What's really on your mind?"

"Our children."

Rosie rested a hand on her stomach. Med techs had confirmed: twins. Granted, they wouldn't be born for another seven months, but their imminence thrilled and terrified Ardan. "The third generation of Verges born on Mars."

"Unless they're born elsewhere."

Her eyes widened. "You want to leave?"

Ardan walked away, to the hab's wall. He pressed a switch, lowering the thick, rubble-covered shutter of their single window. Red-orange light spilled in through the three-meter length, casting their handful of chairs, food processing station, and Rosie's assortment of charcoal-etched landscapes in uniform bloody colors. "This is the only world I've ever known. My family built Ferro Plains from scratch. I could walk the tunnels between habs blindfolded and deaf, and never get lost. But Grandfather was lost in the maelstrom of 'Ninety-Nine, when Dad was just seven. And Dad… the med techs couldn't get the right therapies in place to heal his lungs from dust-rip. At least I was twenty and able to take on his responsibilities. Mars isn't happy we're here, Rosie. It's not going to accommodate us."

He reached for a foldout computer resting on a chair. The screen flashed on, and Ardan swiped through his latest reads. "Look at this."

The planet glowed as a brilliant sapphire jewel, cutting through the reddish gloom. Rosie put her hands to her mouth.

"This is what the Raszewski drive means," Ardan said. "People are leaving Mars, leaving asteroids, flocking to these new planets. It's months or years of travel, but we're talking dozens of light-years away. When you get there, there's no dust, no ES suit, none of that needed. They're other Earths. Think about it. We could start over, be pioneers just like our people were two hundred years ago when they rolled wagons into the Great Plains."

Rosie shook her head. "But Ard, this is home. It's always been home."

"You were right. I do need to take Li's offer." He held her hands. "But when I get paid, we need to consider what 'home' means. This place, where we can struggle and scrape for the next three generations? Or a planet that welcomes us?"

"Take the delivery, but think hard on this, Ard."

"I will." He plucked the communicator from his belt and called up Li's link address. "You should, too."

The next day, he and Tadzio stared out the windows of Li Huan's office at Boreus Prime. The crawler bigger than Ferro Plains, Ardan was willing to bet. He didn't bother reading the specs. Tadzio would have it all memorized. The thing's treads were each longer than five rovers, and it had ten sets.

More impressive was the mountain of ice being slowly dragged onto its back.

"There is enough water locked in that glacier to last a settlement decades." He hadn't heard Li approach, soft as the carpet was. Li wore an immaculate suit of cobalt blue, over a cream shirt with a collar that reached his chin. His hair was slicked to the left. The right was shaved. Red tattoos covered the bare side of his head. "We have to use sonic chisels to break it free of the main mass. Torches would evaporate along the cuts; too much would be wasted."

"What about the slivers that crack off? Those have to be dozens of meters long." Ardan pressed his fingers to the glass, feeling the cold of the Martian evening. He imagined he could touch the glacier itself.

"Utility drones." Li pointed at tiny yellow and black shapes skittering in the wake of the sluggish glacier. "None will go to waste."

"This is the most amazing sight," Tadzio said. "And you want us … to drive this?"

"The crawler is an incredibly expensive and complex piece of machinery, Mr. Mazorwiecki, and as such does not require guidance. It has limited artificial intelligence. It could navigate the whole of Mars by itself. What it needs, though, are people to protect it from … hostile takeover."

"Right. We're driving through Vastitas, so you're expecting raiders," Ardan said.

"Self-defense systems are an added cost the colony administration does not feel justifies expenditure." Li sniffed. "I disagreed, hence my willingness to add security bonuses totaling one hundred fifty thousand to the project."

"We're not mercenaries, Li. You'd be better off hiring the Earth boys in their exoskeletons, if they're not too busy putting down riots on their Moon."

"You've hit upon our quandary. No, neither of you are trained for security, but you are long-time settlers with not only intimate knowledge of the terrain and weather, but the technology. Both of you descend from original American and Polish settlers, two sets of peoples who were key in maintaining the original Martian settlements' infrastructure."

"We are still vital." Tadzio's posture improved by several centimeters. "There is nothing that could run without our expertise."

"I would not flatter yourselves," Li said. "Nevertheless, I need you to make this last venture of mine prosperous, for all our sakes."

"Last?" Ardan frowned. "Don't tell me the Progress Corporation fired you for arguing on the extra expense."

"Not at all. I have been saving for some time to relocate my family." Li smiled. "Surely you're aware of the shipyards churning out huge transports equipped with Raszewski spheres? My family, including that of my sisters, is due to leave in two months."

Ardan felt sick. Li was one of the few not out to completely screw the average settler. Who'd Ferro Plains have left to deal with if he abandoned Mars?

"A moment," Tadzio said. "You said bonus was one hundred fifty thousand, yet you pay Ardan and I fifty apiece for our services. Where is the other third?"

10

"Ah. It is reserved for a local guide." Li touched his collar. A blue light glowed inside the fabric. "Send up Mr. Bidarte."

He said nothing more until the visitor arrived. The man was taller than all three of them, slender, wearing a black and grey exoskeleton that cocooned his entire body. It framed a sickly pale face, yet he didn't seem ill. His jumpsuit was deep vermillion.

"This is Ganix Bidarte," Li said. "From Lore Hotza settlement. He will provide additional security on the route. He's quite familiar with the raiders, as they've targeted his home more than once."

"I have never heard of any successful attacks on a Lore Hotza," Tadzio said.

"None have been successful." Ganix's voice was thick and buzzed with the motors of his exoskeleton. "My clan has made sure of that."

His accent, his pale complexion, the need for an exoskeleton in the office's Earth-normal gravity setting, all marked Ganix as someone who lived without the technology that let other Mars settlers like Ardan and Tadzio maintain their homeworld heritage. Ardan scowled as he realized the connections. "You're a freelander."

"Mars will stay Mars, grav-infant." Ganix made a face, as if he'd stepped in refuse. "Do not pretend to think it your world. You cannot change it."

"Mr. Bidarte's politics aside, he is concerned

for the safety of his settlement." Li's voice brooked no tolerance for dissention. "I remind all three of you that our financial well-being is at stake. Surely there is room for our varied livelihoods on the Red Planet."

Looking at Ganix, the man who refused artificial gravity, Ardan wasn't so sure.

They left early the next morning, with the tiny bright circle of Earth watching them. Ardan squinted though the crawler's control cab windows, until the light detectors polarized the view.

"This will be, as they say, the scenic route." Tadzio clapped Ardan on the back. The dust-brain could have been celebrating retirement.

"Yeah, especially since this thing maxes out at 40 kph." Dust swirled in huge clouds churned up by the monster treads. Ardan walked to the back of the control cab, which was a transparent, 20-meter-wide blister atop the crawler's forward section. Large white shutters of reinforced carbon fiber could be swiveled into place to shield the cab from storms. Ardan used the shutter board to slide the rear segment out of his way, allowing for a clean view of the looming glacier. It gleamed white, a giant tooth reaching into the hazy sky. Majestic.

While we're riding a wart on a toad, he thought.

And not even a single wart, when one counted the radar and LIDAR lumps scattered up the crawler's sloping backside.

"Keep your gaze fixed on the way ahead, not the road behind." Ganix stood surrounded by curved monitor slabs that showed the view transmitted by the crawler's innumerable cameras. He'd shed his exoskeleton and loped with an easy grace under Mars gravity. "Raiders will often circle their prey before striking. Watch for wayward rovers."

"Thanks, we've handled rovers before," Ardan said. "And done pretty well."

"Despite your crippling of yourselves? Quite the achievement."

"If you two children are not going to play nice, I will take away your toys." Tadzio hopped to the other side of the cab and expanded a LIDAR screen. "Nothing but weather-drones in the skies. The track is properly programmed."

"Do you suggest we lounge about, then, like the indolent rich at Boreus?" Ganix reached for a long bundle resting against the back wall of the cab. "I will walk a circuit around the crawler and the glacier. Our radios are linked. Advise me of any interlopers."

"I think we should take a moment to plan our response if we encounter raiders," Tadzio said. "Other than simply watching."

Ganix fitted a breathing mask over his face,

complete with polarized lenses. He unwrapped the bundle, revealing a long, slender rifle. Ardan had never seen one of that design; it didn't fit any models he was familiar with and had a decidedly cobbled-together appearance. Ganix slung it over one shoulder and headed for the airlock.

"Chatty." Tadzio took a swig from a water bottle.

Ardan watched as Ganix used the catwalks toward the back of the crawler, then disappear behind the glacier. "Fanatic."

"So what? If he and his kind want to live their lives without gravity therapy and waste away in the dust, what business is that of ours?" Tadzio grinned. "I for one am still pleased to take Progress's money."

Ardan shook his head. The LIDAR did show everything clear, and the crawler's systems seemed functional, but he wouldn't relax until the week was up. "I've got better things I could be doing. The guys I left at Ferro to run the condensers are good, but if they slip up, I'll be out of touch. Li wouldn't let me give Rosie the crawler's frequency out here. He's afraid of us being tracked."

"It is not as if we'll accidentally run someone over." Tadzio wiped his mouth with the back of his hands. "Come, run diagnostics with me. If you are preoccupied, you will not worry, yes?"

Ardan thought of Rosie, and their twins, and the blue planet. "Sure. No worry."

The third day dawned as numbing as the other two. Ardan woke, did some push-ups—way more than he usually accomplished, thanks to taking exercise in reduced gravity—and walked up the narrow corridor of the bunk cabins to the control cab. A low-level storm was passing by, twenty clicks ahead and to the southwest, but it was moving off, out of the crawler's course. Tadzio was still asleep. He had no idea where Ganix was. Probably off roosting on the glacier.

Ardan ripped open a dried fruit package. The cab radio beeped. "Go ahead."

"I have contacts, east, ten clicks." Ganix's voice was scratchy.

Ardan checked the scope. Yes, the LIDAR picked up robots. "Looks like scouters chasing the storm," he said. "I'll ping their IDs, see if the Mars Weather Institute's running a maelstrom predictor. MWI's always got some weird experiment or another going. Hasn't helped them pinpoint a blasted thing."

"Are you certain?"

"Seen it plenty of times near Ferro Plains."

"Very well." Ganix sounded disappointed. Ardan would be too, if he were on near-constant guard duty on an icy mountain for 72 hours. "Send your ping."

"How about you send me whatever imagery

you've got on your scope."

"Sending." Ganix signed off.

"And hey, how's your morning? It's fine, and yours?" Ardan rolled his eyes. He dragged one of the curved monitors over and accepted the incoming download. It was wobbly, coming as it were from Ganix's scope, but it sufficed.

Ardan frowned as he chewed raisins. Those MWI bots were running a way too straight-line pattern. They should be weaving in and around the trailing edges of the storm, trying to check wind variance, temperature, and the like. Ardan sent the ping, then zoomed in on the image.

Progress Corp utility drones?

"Doesn't make sense," he said aloud.

"Humph? Good morning to you, as well." Tadzio stretched and yawned. "What have we this fine rusty day?"

"Utility bots, playing storm chaser." Ardan showed Tadzio the recording and compare it to the LIDAR readouts.

"That is cheap for MWI," Tadzio murmured. "Have they lost funding to resort to the clunkiest robots on Mars?"

"They have specialized units based on utility bots." Ardan switched scan modes, to infrared, for a reading on their power cores.

The results came back spiked in entirely the wrong wavelength.

"Blast!" Ardan grabbed up the radio. He

fumbled, dropping it to the floor. Fruit spilled across the deck. "Ganix! Ganix, you read?"

"What is it?"

"Those bots! They're weather related. Something's wrong. I'm getting energy readings way out of whack with a circulating battery."

Ganix muttered something in a language Ardan couldn't translate. "They are no longer following the storm."

He was right. The flock of bots wheeled off the storm's trail, less than five clicks away. They swept toward the crawler, kicking streams of orange sand, in an arrow formation of … sixteen? The LIDAR must have missed some.

"*Zepsuty!*" Tadzio was gripping both sides of the screen that showed the scan readouts. "Battery, my foot! Ardan, those bots are rigged with demolition explosives!"

"You're sure?"

"Absolutely! They are same output I employ to clear underground channels."

"Get this thing out of their way!" Ardan hurtled for the passageway. Instead of heading down to the bunks, he clambered up the ladder, taking three rungs at a time.

He emerged into a dark chamber, no bigger than the interior of his rover. He dug for the keys in his pocket and jammed them into the lock.

A 360-degree screen lit up, surrounding him with a gorgeous panoramic view of the burnt landscape. The storm was a churning, monstrous cloud off to one direction. Tendrils of dust marked the oncoming bots.

"Ganix, you with me?" He reached up for a set of handholds.

"I read." Something scraped in the background. "I am seeking higher ground for better targeting. In position, fifteen seconds."

"I'm in the Pod." Ardan yanked on the handholds. A long column dropped from the ceiling. A pair of handles popped from the sides. LIDAR and radar readouts cascaded into view. Camera imagery exploded into view on dozens of panels spread around the Pod.

Ardan plugged the radio into the column and grasped the handles. They conformed to his hands, letting him rest his fingers on the firing studs. Those bots were closing fast. "Tadzio, how're we looking?"

"We would be better if crawler would get off the course and stop lumbering ahead without regard to danger." Tadzio spouted another sentence in Polish that Ardan assumed was extremely derogatory. "I am attempting override. AI is not accepting that utility drones are a threat. I am explaining they carry high explosives. We have slight communications problem."

"What about Progress? Can we get off a distress call?"

"Negative. Our outbound radio is jammed."

"What? From where? The bots?"

"Too small. There is someone else out there, around the storm. I cannot pinpoint. Are you ready?"

"Pod's warmed up. I'm bringing the Gauss guns online."

"Ganix here. I am prepared."

Ardan let the targeting computer bracket the sixteen robots with red highlights. They were near enough now he could see them clearly in enhanced visuals. "Take them out."

He pressed the triggers.

The whole room vibrated, as if he were standing inside a deep core drill. Above him, four of the radar and LIDAR blisters had cracked open. Anyone watching outside would see four weapons emerge, mounted on gimbals, each one with a squared barrel of two pieces. Ardan thought of them as the open mouth of a dragon.

Difference was, these dragons belched magnetically accelerated tungsten rounds.

The Gauss guns tore chunks from the matted plains, leaving blackened gouges where sand swirled. One of the drones exploded, fragments spraying its companions. A ball of fire fizzled out in a puff of thick smoke.

Either the remaining drones had a heightened sense of self-preservation, or their controllers had good reflexes, because the formation broke apart. The arrow became pairs and trios, then single drones, then randomly reformed in groups of varying size. They moved so quickly Ardan was dizzied. He imagined he could hear their motors whirring even through the Pod's walls, and over the buzz saw of the Gauss guns.

Ardan fired into their midst, loosing shot after shot as the turrets rotated for optimal aim. Each hand control was linked to a turret; the targeting system did most of the work as he pointed and shot. Still, these weren't expensive tracking rounds but cheap projectiles. There was only so much he and the guns could do to keep up. The drones were far too agile.

Another drone exploded, followed by a third, then a fourth. "Ganix!" Ardan shouted into the radio. "A little help!"

"Who do you suppose cleared two by himself?"

Two what? Ardan realized a pair of drones headed for the rear of the crawler had been reduced to smoldering smudges on the landscape. A flash of light from the glacier's pinnacle speared another drone, and just like that, the field of targets was reduced to nine.

"Ardan!" Tadzio's voice rang inside the Pod. "I have isolated signal guiding the drones. There are two, perhaps three rovers on the nearest rise. If I can convince the crawler to interpose itself between our adversaries and their robotic slaves, I can cut them off."

"Do it!"

"Only if the festering AI will recognize the threat!"

"Let it know we're fully aware." Ardan wrenched his shoulder swiveling the targeting column to meet four oncoming drones that had abruptly formed a line aiming for the crawler's forward tracks. No sooner had he fired then they shot apart. Ardan managed only to destroy one.

But the crawler turned. Ponderously, achingly slow, but it *turned*. Ardan could see the ridge Tadzio spoke of, disappearing behind the control cab. Just another minute…

Three of the remaining drones rocketed off the ground, hurtling straight for the control cab.

"Tadzio! Get out!" Ardan blasted away at the drones. If they took out the cab, it wouldn't matter what course they set, the crawler would creep to a halt—or worse, continue right into the path of the raiders hidden up on the ridge.

"No! Concentrate your fire on the main group!" Ganix's ordered buffeted Ardan, but he ignored him, expending ammo until the first of the three airborne drones exploded, then the second—

The third blew up between the Pod and the cab. Tadzio's cries pierced Ardan's hearing, then cut off in a squeal of static. Black smoke swept across his screens. The concussion rattled the entire forward section of the crawler. Ardan lost his grip on the targeting column. He grazed his knees on the deck.

"Verge!" Ganix's weapon howled in the background on the radio channel. "Grav-infant!"

"Shut up and finish off those drones!" Ardan dragged himself upright, squinting at the screens as LIDAR did its best to highlight the last few—

The crawler bucked like Ardan's rover when Tadzio launched it over a steep rise. Ardan maintained his grip on the control column. He'd never surfed—imagine, water so vast you could *ride* it!—but that must have been a similar sensation. His stomach rose into his throat.

Everything ground to a halt.

When the smoke finally cleared, Ardan saw crater after crater where his and Ganix's shots had destroyed drones. He also saw the control cab, intact, but with fractures across the armored shutters.

"Ganix, what can you see from up there?" Ardan slid down the ladder, slamming into the deck below. He sprinted toward the cab. Tadzio's sister lived in New Warsaw. How was he going to tell her?

"The middle left tread assembly is wrecked." Ice crunched underfoot. Ganix must be on his way down off the glacier. "There's damage to the rear left, too. I cannot tell how much."

"Let me see what the crawler says. Meantime, you stay out there and watch our buddies on the hill."

"They are not moving. I will inspect the damage at closer range."

"Ganix, what did I just say?"

"Nothing I should heed." The signal cut.

"Blast!" Ardan slung open the hatch to the control cab. Smoke poured out. He gasped for air. Tadzio was sprawled on the floor, groaning. The smoke wasn't rushing for him but was being drawn away.

Red lights flashed. Hull breach.

Ardan stepped over Tadzio. The seriousness of his injuries would be moot if all their air got sucked out. Mars offered them nothing to breathe.

Fortunately, the armored sheathing outside had clamped down, sealing as tight as it could, even with a jagged, narrow crack running as long as his arm. Ardan swept a hand torch and a slab of atmo-caulk from an aid kit tucked beside the hatch. The atmo-caulk exploded into a gooey mess along the crack, bubbling where the two air pressures interacted. He ran the torch's hot purple flare over the edges, quickly as he dared, without leaving a hole.

Bubbles ceased. Ardan took deep, slow breaths.

The lights flashed to orange, then green, before resuming their normal pale-yellow hue.

Ardan sagged to the deck. Sweat stung his eyes. He reached over and slapped Tadzio on the back.

"Ow." Tadzio pushed onto his side.

"Anything broken?"

"Only my pride, I think." He winced. "And possibly my right wrist."

The imagery on the crawler's cameras showed Ganix's assessment was spot on. The middle tread on the left side was torn to strips and blackened. The one behind it was crumpled.

Ganix's scope showed the wreckage more clearly.

"We do not have the facilities to repair such damage at Lore Hotza," he said, "Nor do we have the correct parts to fabricate. We will have to contact Boreus."

"Which I would happily do, if not for jamming." Tadzio gingerly touched the radio, taking care that the splint around his wrist didn't move too quickly. "Whatever is being done, is better than I can manage."

"If you had been worth your weight in coddled flesh, you could have stopped the remote signal for the drones."

"Hey, take it easy." Ardan stepped between them. "Tadzio did his best."

"No. He was incompetent. As were you."

"Incompetent? I think someone forgot how to count. You saw how many drones I blasted away from us."

"Yet you fell for the ruse. While you protected

the cab, our attackers stopped the crawler. All we can do is sit and wait for them to pick the skin from our bones at their leisure."

"Oh?" Tadzio pushed by Ardan. "And where were your vaunted skills? You are the special liaison we had to take. Some help. You hide on your ice rock and sneer at the people working to improve this planet, all so you can play desert dweller. Call yourself a native. You cannot even survive without the ice we bring!"

"I would slit you from your waist to your chin if I thought you worth the effort."

"That's enough!" Ardan pushed them apart. "Ganix, make yourself useful and find get the crawler's repair functions running. If we can get it moving again, we might still make it to your settlement. Move it!"

Ganix stalked through the airlock, and Ardan was never more mindful of the giant rifle he carried. So. Repair. The crawler's computer made their situation painfully obvious: while there was indeed extra track aboard, parts needed to replace the wheels inside the damaged portion weren't available.

"Look at this section." Tadzio tapped a display depicting the entire vehicle. "If we can cut through the broken track assembly, then repurpose part of the right side, we may be able to get underway."

"Maybe. And not likely before the raiders board us." Ardan glanced at the horizon. No moves yet. Why should they hurry? "Probably waiting to see if our life-support fails. I'll go see what we can salvage. Keep trying to break through the jamming."

"Ardan, wait." Tadzio rubbed his wounded wrist. "Thank you for saving my life."

"I've always had your back."

"But you are leaving."

"The cab?"

"Mars."

Ardan grimaced. "I didn't want to spring it on you, but I kept running out of times and places to bring it up. I suppose Rosie let it slip."

"Not at all. I asked her, and she confirmed." Tadzio smiled ruefully. "She made me swear to keep my trap shut, I believe were the instructions."

"This place isn't home for me, Tadzio. It never has been. No matter how much Grandpa and Dad wanted it. It's sucked our family's resources dry. I want something better for the twins, when they come. I want them to have a home that won't keep them in poverty, where the land itself won't tolerate life. Out there, those new planets light-years away, there's opportunity."

Tadzio nodded. "I understand, I think. Mars has been the only place for such a long time. Suddenly, we have new frontiers, frontiers that can be visited with nothing but the most basic supplies and the clothes upon our backs. But you would abandon the people who depend on your support?"

"I don't want to argue the point. If they want to stay and survive, that's fine. But I'm done surviving. I have to improve."

"Do not throw away all that our people have done here, Ard. What about the community you have built here?"

Ardan donned his ES suit. "Everything the Verges have built can be buried in a single maelstrom."

The crawler was equipped with six Heavy Repair Drones, each one a lumbering spider half the size of Ardan's rover. He followed two of them as they skittered down the side of the glacier, tracking their progress from the crisscrossing stairs and ladders that led several stories to the ground.

One of the spiders used plasma torches to cut away the wreckage, while its companion bent metal and extruded temporary adhesive. None of the scraps were wasted. Ardan directed their operations, making sure they were following the plans he'd programmed. They made good time dismantling part of the extra tracks from the right side, but when it came to fitting them on the left, kept bumping up against wiring that operated coolant systems in the aft quarter of the crawler.

"Just bypass them!" Ardan slapped one of the HRD legs, fully aware it would not respond to physical provocation, or his outburst. The problem was, safety protocols prohibiting endangering vital systems. But Ardan knew the specs—there was precious little else to study on their drive out. So, he knew there was a three-minute gap in which the wiring could be rerouted before the cooling dropped below critical levels.

Try convincing an HRD.

"Mechanical beasts are as temperamental as live ones." Ganix crouched high above, on the shroud covering the damaged track assembly.

"You could help, instead of perching." Ardan polarized the ES suit's faceplate and pried loose the coupling for the coolant wires. He started a timer for three minutes on his displays. He was sweating, surly, and to top it all, his rad count was at 70 percent. He'd have to finish the work and spend time inside the insulated control cab if he was going to stay below the recommended daily exposure. "Sever these anchors so we can clear the wiring."

Ganix leapt down, the impact of his landing as graceful as a solstice dancer in Ferro's community hall. He used his own torch to cut the anchors on one end of the coupling, while Ardan did likewise. The HRD stood nearby, awaiting instruction— sulking, Ardan imagined.

"You've never even seen a real animal," Ardan muttered. "Never even left the planet."

"I have not. Have you?"

Ardan cut the last anchor and dragged the half-meter thick bundle of cabling back. He sent the command to the HRD to get the new frame into place.

"This is not your usual occupation," Ganix said.

"Lucky guess?"

"I queried your background when Lore Hotza made this arrangement with Progress Corporation. You run Ferro Plains settlement."

"Run is an exaggeration."

"The people follow your lead. Even so, they depart."

Ardan's timer had a minute left. The HRD was nearly finished. "Can't make them do what they don't want, Ganix, not with Progress squeezing them for everything they earn. Sixty years of trying to make Mars better, some people don't have much to show for it."

"They fail because they try to change Mars."

"Can't survive elsewise."

"Is that so? My people have managed. We do not force Mars to change the way it breathes. We do not huddle around gravity generators. This is our home. We must adapt to it, not the reverse."

"Sure. Then we'd be stuck here, never able to visit Earth or the space-borne settlements." The HRD backed away. Ardan slammed the cabling home into the coupling. He blew out a breath. He'd have liked to open his faceplate for a cool breeze.

Cool breeze? Had he ever felt such a thing? Once. Dad took him to Earth, when he was six. Face-to-face trade, for tech to be used at Ferro. Ardan closed his eyes. Breezes. Unfiltered air. And rain.

"Why would you ever return to the cesspool of humanity? Here we are better. Our existence is pure." Ganix waved his hand around. "Mars has all we need."

"It doesn't have everything I need. My children should grow up to be people who can go anywhere, do anything," Ardan said. "They stay here, they'll either never be able to leave, or they'll be trapped in their own prison."

"This is why our world will wait for us of the free lands long after you have abandoned it."

Ardan leaned against the crawler. "Maybe you can have it, then. Meantime, we've got to figure out a solution to our raider problem."

"How so?"

Tadzio had sent Ardan imagery from the LIDAR feeds, which Ardan passed along to Ganix's link. Rovers were on the move, coming down the long, shallow slope of the ridge's far side. "I don't think they're coming to inspect the damage."

"Likely they mean to kill the three of us and take the ice."

"My guess too."

Ganix unlimbered his rifle. It hummed in anticipation of another fight. "Let them try."

"Hang on. We're not going to repel another frontal assault, not considering all the damage we sustained."

"You have a solution?"

Ardan peered up at the Gauss guns. The mounts were jammed. "Yeah. Yeah, I do."

The three men hunkered down and watched from concealment for the approaching rovers. When the motley assortment of vehicles was five klicks out, it started snowing.

Ardan had only seen it once before, as a teen. The moisture hammered diagonally, driving sheets of ice that covered his faceplate. The sleet subsided in half a minute, and when it passed, a silvery sheen draped everything. Five minutes later, it all vanished, evaporating in the thin atmosphere.

It didn't improve the looks of the convoy, even though it slowed their approach. Ten rovers fanned out in similar formation to that employed by the explosive-carrying drones. None appeared standard models; some had double cockpits, others jury-rigged projectile weapons, still more hauling crates. Ammunition? Food and water? None were labeled.

Ardan wanted that one.

"Remember," Tadzio murmured into the radio. "I've modified the HRD's programming as much as it will allow. You'll have less than a minute before the safety protocols kick in and it drops the load."

"Got it. And good work."

"Thank me only if my signal gets through their jamming, my friend."

Ganix's voice cut across their feed, static-filled. "In position. I have one vehicle marked for you. Its energy output far exceeds the others.""

A red outline traced one of the two double-cockpit rovers. "Good as guess as any. Tadzio?"

"Yes. Yes, that should be it. I will be ready."

"Good. We'll only get one shot at this, gentlemen." Ardan loaded an image of Rosie, resting on a lounger in their home, reading. Martin sun lit her orange-gold. "Make it count."

He cut off their signal. Watched as the rovers encircled the crawler. They sent six vehicles around the undamaged side, the side which they knew the Gauss guns couldn't reach because they were jammed in their mounts.

Ardan waited until the heaviest laden truck stopped. He could see figures in mottled grey-red ES suits disembarking.

He'd rather have a stationary target, anyway.

The HRD on which he sat like a cavalry steed of old clambered over the top of the Pod, amidst the domes. It grasped a dismantled Gauss gun in four arms. Ardan had the power supply rigged to the HRD's batteries. An ammunition belt strung all the way back to the gimbals from which he'd detached it.

A tiny suited figure pointed his way.

Ardan opened fire.

Blasts cratered the plains, obscuring his view for only a moment, until the blasts hit the heavy rover. It exploded in a huge ball of fire, blindingly bright. The shockwave toppled two of the nearby mounts. Suited figures scattered.

Then they shot back.

Projectiles winged the crawler's hide and sent sprays of ice from the glacier. Ardan ducked behind the HRD, holding the improvised trigger. The last of the ammunition clanged across the deck, bouncing toward the Gauss gun. In twenty seconds, he'd be out, and the HRD would be a dead target, never mind its programming.

A second rover exploded, but it wasn't the one broadcasting the jamming. By then the raiders reached the crawler treads. Ardan urged the HRD forward, firing the last of the Gauss rounds. Then he gave it a last command: clean the sides of the crawler.

The HRD dropped the Gauss gun and skittered along the hull, spraying a thick foam over every surface it encountered. Thanks to Tadzio's mucking about with its internal memory, its normal guidelines to safeguard nearby humans were a tad fuzzy. Several raiders lost their grip on climbing tethers and fell back to the sands. But a well-placed explosive ripped the poor HRD in half, spilling its innards.

Its ersatz death both saddened and puzzled Ardan. Funny, putting so much faith and a sense of camaraderie in some collection of circuits and wires.

He didn't have time to ruminate on the philosophical aspects before the first raiders crested the crawler's upper deck.

Ardan appeared from behind one of the LIDAR domes, charging the intruder. He put his back onto the dome, planted his boots on the man's chest, and shoved. He flew backwards, arms flailing in panicked frenzy for a handhold.

The next two were armed, and faster. One of them shot Ardan, the bullet ripping the right shoulder of his ES suit. Air hissed out. Red lights rimmed his vision. Hopefully the self-sealant still worked, or he'd be passing out in the middle of this fight. Ardan pushed the thought out of his mind as he went for the attacker's knees.

They went tumbling across the deck, forcing the next assailant to hop-skip over them. As he did, Ardan dug for the Hunsaker P60 pistol concealed under his suit belt. Two shots hit the man mid-air, blood spattering on the LIDAR dome.

Ardan rolled with his attacker and clubbed his visor with the pistol until air hissed through a crack. Red lights faded to amber, then green as his own suit stopped its leak. But the bandit was smart enough to drive a blow at Ardan's wounded shoulder. Pain stabbed through the gunshot, and before he knew it, Ardan found himself staring down the muzzle of his own gun.

A shot boomed from far of. There was a flash, and a ragged hole, the edges burnt and smoking, appeared in the raider's chest. He toppled like a statue.

More gunshots, like distant thunder, rolled over the plains. The raiders climbing up the side scrambled either to get to the top or retreated to the bottom. They weren't fast enough, most. Ganix's abilities as a sniper chilled Ardan. He picked them off one by one.

An explosion sent a column of smoke from the opposite side of the crawler. Tadzio came hustling around the LIDAR domes and defunct Gauss turrets. "Ardan! You are hurt."

"Not dead, so there's a plus."

"They are still climbing the left side," Tadzio said. "I am afraid my explosive intervention only slowed them."

"Better than nothing." Three more raiders clambered onto the deck. "Got your torch?"

"Of course. And a friend." Tadzio had an identical Hunsaker pistol.

Shots filled the air as they hunkered among the domes, fending off the remaining raiders. Ganix continued to drop their attackers, one at a time, leaving their opponents hesitant.

Ganix sent Ardan imagery from his scope. The raiders who'd fallen were regrouping. They headed for their rovers, on either side of the crawler. "If they are allowed to seek shelter and rearm, we will not be able to stop them."

"Then we do Plan B." Ardan scooted between domes. A gunshot ricocheted off the deck. "Tadzio! Light the charges."

"Right with you!" Tadzio primed his torch, well beyond the safe level for cutting output. "Ganix! Now is the time!"

"Throw it."

Tadzio flung the device. It glowed hot pink and purple as it activated.

A gunshot boomed. The flare was blinding, so much so Ardan grimaced even with the polarization of his faceplate, but he slammed his hand down on the trigger hidden at the base of the same ruined Gauss gun mount he'd jury-rigged. Tadzio did likewise.

Charges interspersed around the sides of the glacier rumbled, shearing of huge blades of ice. They hurtled down the slopes, picking up more fragments. Twin avalanches crashed onto the rovers, smashing them beneath tons of ice.

Tadzio whooped. "The jamming has ceased! Sending our emergency signal."

The last raiders retreated down the sides of the crawler. Tadzio hurried from his hiding place, but Ardan grabbed his arm. "Don't bother. No point getting ourselves killed while they're running."

"But we cannot let them escape!"

One of the small, ES-suited figures sprinting over the ice fell, then another. Ardan felt sick, but the alternative was his death, and that of his friend. Would he trade the lives of these desert bandits for his own, so that his unborn children would have a father?

Absolutely.

"Ganix has it in hand," Ardan said. "Let's clean up."

Progress sent their private security forces swooping in, broad-winged aircraft trailing huge shadows over the crawler cab. They found eight men to arrest. Eight, of thirty.

More repair drones showed up, as well as a platoon of HRDs. It took thirty-six hours to get the crawler up and running. The techs admitted to Ardan it would have been longer but for the repairs he had already affected.

By the time they reached the Lore Hotza settlement, Ardan longed for Ferro Plains and its cantankerous condensers.

Ganix saw them off as they boarded a Progress aircraft for the return. "You have done our people a great service. I thank you."

Ardan shook his hand. "You understand why I make the choices I do, right? I don't want my children—or myself—to be at a disadvantage when it comes to any other human settling this galaxy."

Ganix nodded. "I do understand. You, Ardan Verge, strive to be one of many. I sweat and bleed to be strong among few. It is not worth the pain to be weak. I am content to be a Martian."

They made the delivery to Lore Hotza and the return trip to Boreus without incident. Even the storms held off, as if Mars was content to allow the settlement's prosperity grow.

Ardan shook his head. He was sounding like Ganix.

Back at Boreus, in the cushy confines of the Progress office, Li Huan poured them a fizzing champagne. "The last of my stock. I couldn't bear to leave it behind for my successor, not when it accompanied my grandfather on his journey to Mars. There's simply not the room for it on our new trek."

"Good luck to you and your family." Ardan took a sip. The champagne stung his cracked, parched lips, but the flavor soothed his throat.

"Congratulations on defending the crawler."

"Thank you." Tadzio drained his glass, as if he'd forgotten it wasn't a shot of vodka. He sighed deeply. "We would very much appreciate the money in lieu of thanks."

"Of course." Li reached for a black case on his desk. He applied his middle three fingers of his left hand. A sensor beeped and it popped open. Stacks of Martian scrip filled the case, identical squares of red designs with silver and black edging.

Not enough, though.

"If that is supposed to be fifty thousand for each of us, I suggest you have your accountant do a recount," Tadzio muttered.

Li's constant smile waned. "It is out of my hands, gentlemen. Unfortunately, the Progress board of directors was less than pleased with the collateral damaged caused in repelling the bandits. Twenty thousand has been deducted from your respective contracts."

Ardan stared at Li.

"There was nothing I could do." Li sighed. "With my departure, the board has begun to push me out of its deliberations. I daresay my replacement already has gained considerable influence."

"I understand." Ardan set his unfinished champagne on the desk. He input his fingerprints into the security program and locked the case. "You have other priorities."

"Yes. My family."

Ardan offered his hand. "Good luck to you."

"Clear skies, Ardan Verge." Li shook.

Ardan and Tadzio found themselves out in the corridor, gazing out the windows at another looming mountain of ice. Who would drive that one through the wastes? How many drones would be lost? How much more would Progress take from the dwindling supply of people willing to eke out a living on Mars?

"Well," Tadzio said. "At least now, our options are clearer."

"They are."

"Do you know where you'll go?"

"Rosie has family connections. But… This has been our life. Where else is there?"

"A slew of worlds, my friend." Tadzio clapped a hand on his shoulder. "Wherever you want to go that is not the dust death of Mars or the corrupt chaos of Earth."

"What about you?"

Tadzio shrugged. "My people have a new flower of a planet on which they have already set up camps. It will be a rough frontier, yes, but a breathable one."

Ardan nodded. They had decisions to make, for their lives and those unborn.

Rosie clung to him for what seemed like an hour as soon as he returned to their hab. "Word of the attack reached me a day ago. Are you okay?"

"No permanent damage. Dings and scratches." Ardan took her hands in his. "Rosie, the contract fee—"

"I know. It's not enough to meet the sixty-year mark."

"But it's more than plenty for the alternative."

"I've been thinking... We wouldn't be alone."

"I hate to abandon this place, but if our children want to grow up with their father—with a father who can be around for their grandchildren, it's a simple choice."

"I know. I'll start the account transfers."

"And I'll inform the settlement council. If no one takes on the contract, Ferro Plains is done."

"Someone will." She headed for the computer.

Ardan watched the dust clouds churn. Rusty tendrils blotted out an anemic sun. "Someone always does."

Six months later, he held Rosie's hand as the colony ship *Starkweather* arrived at a temperate world orbiting the Tau Ceti star. Golden sun draped cottony clouds, and endless cobalt oceans. His heart accelerated. The journey was over.

"We're here." He whispered it to Rosie, but also to their children, mere weeks away from birth. The med techs weren't worried, so he figured he shouldn't be either.

"I can see our freeholding." Rosie pointed at the monitor. Her finger obscured a tiny patch of a long, jagged coastline along the second largest continent. "There."

Home. And Ardan couldn't taste a bit of dust.

Visit

www.steverzasa.com

for more adventures in
The Face of the Deep universe

www.ingramcontent.com/pod-product-compliance
Lightning Source LLC
Chambersburg PA
CBHW070943120726
47908CB00005BA/1506